FEATHERSTONE
Bloomsbury Publishing Plc
50 Bedford Square, London, WC1B 3DP, UK
29 Earlsfort Terrace, Dublin 2, Ireland

BLOOMSBURY, FEATHERSTONE and the Feather logo are trademarks of Bloomsbury Publishing Plc

First published in Great Britain 2021 by Bloomsbury Publishing Plc
Text copyright © Penny Tassoni, 2021
Illustrations copyright © Mel Four, 2021

Penny Tassoni and Mel Four have asserted their rights under the Copyright, Designs and Patents Act,
1988, to be identified as Author and Illustrator of this work

A catalogue record for this book is available from the British Library

ISBN: HB: 978-1-4729-7804-2; ePDF: 978-1-4729-7803-5; ePub: 978-1-4729-7805-9

2 4 6 8 10 9 7 5 3 1

Printed and bound in China by Leo Paper Products, Heshan, Guangdong

To find out more about our authors and books visit www.bloomsbury.com and sign up for our newsletters

Time to Get Dressed

Penny Tassoni

Illustrated by Mel Four

FEATHERSTONE

LONDON   OXFORD   NEW YORK   NEW DELHI   SYDNEY

Everyone

wears
clothes...

...and shoes.

There are clothes
that keep you warm.

And clothes that keep you dry.

What do you wear
when it's raining?

There are clothes
for hot weather.

And clothes for sleep.

What do you like to wear to bed?

Clothes and
shoes go on...

And off!

Which of these can you take off by yourself?

Dressing can be fun.

But there's lots to learn.

Can you match pairs of socks and shoes?

Some clothes go on first.

Can you find what goes on next?

Can you
spot what
went on last?

Clothes have fronts and backs.

Which are the fronts
of these clothes?

Trousers can be tricky.

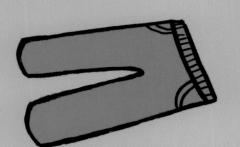

Put them on the floor so you can see the front.

One leg in...
then the other.

Stand up and pull!

Some clothes go over your head.

Which of these do you have?

Lay your top out so you
can see the back.

Pop your head in and pull down.

Then find
the arms...   one by one.

You may need help with zips, buttons and buckles.

But keep on trying because one day...

You will be able to do it
all by yourself!

Notes for parents and carers

Dressing is a skill that is important for children's overall development. It helps develop physical skills such as hand-eye coordination, balance and spatial awareness. Dressing skills are also important for children's confidence and sense of competence. At four years old most children can manage a variety of clothes, although they may still need a little help with fastenings. There are many ways that you can help your child with this skill.

- Build dressing and undressing into daily routines. Allow enough time so that it doesn't become stressful for either of you.

- Start off by encouraging your child to take off items either fully or partially, e.g. hats, unfastened coats. Praise your child's effort even if they need help or get in a muddle.

- Avoid intervening if your child is happy, even if they are making a mistake. Offer help if your child is looking frustrated.

- Encourage your child to collect the clothes that they will be wearing.

- Talk to your child about the features of clothes such as sleeves, collars and buttons.

- Point out the front and back of garments by using clues such as labels.

- Point out the openings in garments, e.g. 'this large hole in the T-shirt is where you put your head'.

- Lay out garments in the order that they need to be put on.

- Sitting on the floor to put on shoes, socks, trousers and tops is often easier for children at first.

- Point out how zips, buttons and buckles work as you are doing them up.

Finally, when buying clothes and shoes, look out for items that will be easy to put on so your child can become increasingly independent.